RAS

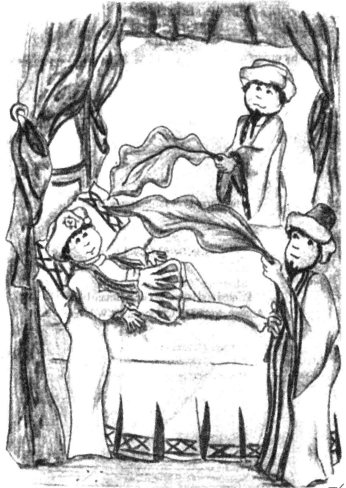

E.R. REILLY

PUBLISHED IN GREAT BRITAIN BY
SATIGO PRESS
PO BOX 8808
BIRMINGHAM
B302LR
E-mail for orders and enquiries: santiago@reilly19.freeserve.co.uk

ISBN 0-9539229-4-4

Reprint 2008, 2010, 2011, 2012

Printed & bound in India by
Authentic India, P.O. Box 2190, Secunderabad 500 003, A.P. - India
E-mail: printing@ombooks.org

Janet would like to dedicate this book to her daughter Jayne - with love as always.

A long, long time ago, there lived a very rich prince. He lived in a huge palace with gold and silver ornaments everywhere. He had riches beyond the wildest dreams of ordinary boys and girls. The rooms in his palace were very big indeed and the ceilings were high enough for a giant to walk around in them with comfort.

The prince was called Rashnu. He wore big baggy shorts with silver and gold stitched into them. He had gold slippers that curled up at the front.

His waistcoat had real diamonds and pearls on it and his turban held a special jewel as big as your hand.

Rashnu had servants for everything. He had servants that would bring him food on big gold plates. He had servants that would bring him a bowl of scented water sprinkled with rose petals just so that he could wash his hands. He had servants to help him get dressed in the morning and servants to help him get undressed at

night and he had any number of servants to wait on him in between.

Every morning the servants would parade in front of him. They would bow their heads and wait for their instructions. Rashnu often asked them to play games with him. Of course they did their best, but they really weren't much fun. They just didn't know how to play. They had never played games themselves. Even as children they had had to work. They were made to work

from when they were very young indeed. Even before they were six years old, they were put to work doing jobs like gathering wood for the fire and fetching water from the well in the village.

Rashnu spent a lot of time lying on his big four poster bed. He had servants who used to stand by the side of the bed waving giant feathers to keep him cool. The problem with Rashnu was that he was bored. There were no other children for him to play with in the palace. Rashnu dreamt about leaving his life behind.He saw himself floating around the world on a flying carpet.

He dreamt that he was flying over

the sea and looking at pirates.

He dreamt that he was on his flying carpet looking at musketeers.

He dreamt that he could see

children racing camels.

He imagined that he was looking

down at all the animals of the jungle

and, best of all, he imagined himself

flying up to the moon.

Rashnu was the richest boy in the whole wide world but he was lonely.

The idea that his father, the King, would let him play with any children who were not from the royal household was, quite frankly, ridiculous. Rashnu never met anyone from outside of the palace. He knew very little about life beyond the palace walls because he was very seldom allowed beyond them. Whenever he was sent to visit outside of the palace it was usually on some holy day or other and he would be sent to one of the great temples in his land. Such visits never really cured his curiosity about the outside world because Rashnu was made to travel in royal style. He sat in a box that had velvet cushions and thick velvet curtains and servants carried him around in it. He never got to see anything of his land but he loved the sounds and smells of the market place. He longed to pull back the curtains and

see who was making all of the noise but he knew he mustn't, it was forbidden. It had been explained to Rashnu that his position in life meant that he should remain removed from ordinary people and that the ways of such folk should remain a mystery to him, just as the ways of royal life should remain a mystery to all but a chosen few.

The long, hot summer days passed slowly for Rashnu, his lessons were boring and he didn't take to schoolwork much. His teachers were wise old men, but nothing that they said held any interest for him. His mind flitted from fancy to fancy. He could never really

concentrate on the dry lifeless history lessons that he was made to endure.

Once a week, he would be granted an audience with his father, the King. His heart leapt with joy whenever their meetings drew near. He loved his father with all of his heart and the weekly meetings were the best part of his week. His teachers would lead the way and Rashnu would follow behind them. They walked up the long aisle that led to where the King sat in waiting on his throne. The teachers would bow down before him and walk backwards to the side of the room leaving Rashnu to stand before him. The King always smiled when he set his eyes upon Rashnu. All of the servants told Rashnu that the weekly meetings made the King smile more than anything else. Rashnu was asked by the King to talk about his lessons and Rashnu would recite all of the facts and figures that he had learnt

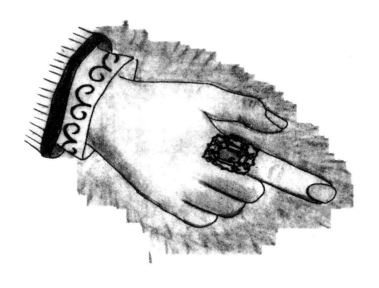

that week. This pleased the King greatly and he would hold his hand out for Rashnu to come forward.

The young prince would kneel down before the King and kiss his royal ring.

The King was pleased with his son and sometimes stroked the young prince's cheek or held his chin in his hand. The servants, too, looked forward to the weekly meetings because they knew that it always put the King in a good mood.

Rashnu was a good son. He seldom got to meet his mother or any of the Kings other wives. He never got to meet his sisters, and he had no brothers, but he remained a good son.

He understood that his position meant that he had responsibilities in life and he was determined to make his father proud of him.

Rashnu would never knowningly have done anything to upset his father, but one day, he was out walking around the grounds of the palace, when he overheard some children playing on the other side of the palace walls. He wanted to shout out to them to say hello and ask them if he could come and play with them. It was no use though, no matter how much his heart yearned to play with the children from the village, he knew that it could never be so. His heart sank as he listened to them running and playing and laughing. Now that he was so close to them he felt lonelier than ever. He decided to go back and lie on his bed. Even though he would be alone there, he wouldn't be tormented by the sounds of children playing.

As he made his way up the great
stone steps back to the palace, a
daring thought came into his mind. He
had never walked up the steps to the
roof of the palace. They were a long
way up and he was not allowed to climb
them. It was far too dangerous, but
he thought to himself that if he were
to climb up there this once, he would
be able to look out over the palace
walls and he would see what it was like
for children who were allowed to run

and play games, to laugh and have fun. His heart began to beat faster as he decided whether to sneak up the steps or to go back to the safety of his room. He knew which was the right choice to make, but the lure of the roof and the freedom that it would give him was too much. He looked all around him, to see if there was anybody watching him. He couldn't see or hear anybody. He thought about his father and how angry he would be

if he found out. He didn't want to

upset his father, and the thought of

being banished from his weekly meeting with him filled Rashnu with sorrow. He stood on the step looking around him in confusion.

He took a deep breath and held his golden slippers in his hand. It was too late. He could hold himself back no longer. Before he knew it his feet were tiptoeing up the old stone steps around the outside of the palace wall and he was on his way up to the roof to look out on the world that was such a mystery to him.

When Rashnu reached the top, he

closed his eyes and took his first deep

breath of free air. He opened up his eyes to look out over the village that was so near to the palace. He could see the people walking along beside donkeys loaded with belongings. He could see women and children queuing up at the well and walking back to their dwellings with large pots of water balanced on their heads.

Best of all, he could see the children playing by the trees near the palace wall. There were lots of

children waiting for a turn on a swing.

It was a rope and a piece of wood that

had been tied to a tree. A man stood

near them, lifting them up onto the piece of wood and pushing them higher and higher. The more they laughed and screamed the higher he pushed them. Rashnu leant on the wall on top of the palace and stared in delight. It looked such fun and he thought to himself that he would give anything to be there with them.

In the distance Rashnu could hear a servant calling his name. He knew that he mustn't be caught there. He raced down the steps to get back into the garden before the servant discovered where he had been. In his haste to get back to the garden he left his golden slippers behind. He was half way down the steps before he realised. He had to decide whether to go back and get them or try to get down to the garden. He decided to go down to the garden. He would just have to say that he had taken them off and left them somewhere. He ran on down the steps towards the garden but, as he ran, he realised that this plan was useless. All of the servants would be ordered to look for them and they would never give up until they were found. He had no choice; he turned round and ran back up to the roof. He could hear the servant calling him, louder now. "Rashnu, Rashnu," his voice rang around the royal grounds. Soon there were other servants shouting his name. He knew that he would have to think and move quickly. If he were caught there, his servants would be ordered to stay with him every minute of the day. His life would be intolerable and he knew that he would never get to see the children from the village playing again. Rashnu looked down from the roof. He could see several of his servants now. They were walking around the garden calling his name. He had no time to lose. He started running down the big steps as quickly and as quietly as he could. As he raced from the bottom step he ran straight into one of the servants. "Whoa, whoa young master. You should not be running so. It is forbidden. It is dangerous to run in the palace grounds." The prince said that he was sorry but there was a flying insect that was chasing him. The young prince was taken indoors, whilst the servants peered all around them, searching for flying insects. They looked a picture

staring in the air with their nets in their hands.

Rashnu had thought quickly and a

good job it was too. He had never before done anything that might upset the King and he was glad – very glad – that he had not been caught.

The long days of Rashnu's young life passed in a slow and consistent way. From time to time he had heard children playing on the swing just a short distance from the palace wall. On more than one occasion he raced up the steps to look out upon them from the palace roof. The fear of getting caught diminished, as he grew increasingly more comfortable with his deceit. Sometimes, though, he grew sad when he thought of how angry the King would be if he were caught. Rashnu thought of a plan that would make it easier for him to escape to the roof. He told his teachers that now he was growing older he wanted time to be alone so that he could spend it in meditation and prayer. His teachers were delighted to grant him his wish. They told the servants to leave him alone when he asked for permission to go into the garden to pray. The King got to find out about his son's request and was very pleased indeed. At their next weekly meeting the King added a very special gem to Rashnu's turban. Rashnu already had a jewel in his turban, but this was bigger and better. In fact, it was the biggest and most expensive jewel in the world. It was a gem that had been given to

the King by his father. It was a family

heirloom that was more precious than

all of the other precious jewels in the

palace put together. It was a mark of

respect from the King to his son and

heir. Rashnu was delighted to have

pleased his father so. When he stopped to think about the real reason that he wanted to be alone he felt really quite guilty, but no amount of guilt could stop him from sneaking away to the roof to watch the village children at play. He saw them jumping around and climbing trees. He saw the man that played with them pushing them higher and higher.

One day, he saw the man climb the tree with a big pot of water strapped to his back. When he got to the top he poured it over the children waiting below. They screamed and laughed as the water sprayed all over them. Rashnu laughed along with them. It was the most fun he had ever seen in his life. Rashnu loved to look out at the children and imagine that he was one of them, laughing and playing alongside them.

One day, as he looked around his secret world, he noticed some of the children from the village playing down by the far end of the palace gardens. Rashnu had never been down there because it was thick with trees. The village children had clung on to some branches that had hung down over the wall. They climbed up the branches and played, climbing around the trees. After a few minutes, they clambered back onto the wall and swung down off the branches back onto their own side. Rashnu was breathless with excitement. The world that he lived in and the world he looked out on had crossed over. If the children of the village could get into his world then this meant that he could get into theirs. It would be easy. Within a few short minutes, he could be free to climb out and meet all of the people he had only managed to look at from a distance.

Rashnu made himself put all of these wicked thoughts from his mind.

He went back to his room and stayed there for the rest of the day. When the servants came to escort him to his evening meal he sent them away. He told them that he wouldn't be eating that day because he wasn't hungry. Really though, he wasn't eating that day because he was punishing himself for having such bad thoughts.

At first, Rashnu allowed himself only to listen to the children. He told himself that he would never again climb the forbidden steps. He promised himself that he would stay where he belonged but it was a promise that he couldn't keep. He couldn't control himself. His feet just climbed the steps by themselves and once again he found himself staring out into the land of fun and laughter. The children from the village had grown braver and were now making regular visits into the palace grounds. Rashnu could see them sneaking around from tree to tree. He saw them venture as far as the fruit trees. The children sat and ate the fruit and laughed quietly as the fresh juice ran down their chins. Rashnu had never climbed a tree before, let alone eaten fruit picked straight off a branch.

When the children from the village returned during the next day, Rashnu was waiting for them. He had walked down to the trees and had climbed one. He sat on a branch, waiting for them to come. When they did come, they were surprised to see him. Rashnu had planned everything he was going to say.

He had left his golden slippers in a safe place; he put his waistcoat with them and turned his trousers and his turban inside out, so that the jewels and the fine gold lace could not be seen. When the children from the village came face to face with him, they were shocked and startled. He told them not to be afraid. He said that he was the son of one of the servants in the palace and he asked them if he could play with them. They weren't sure at first. They thought that he might tell on them and get them into trouble, but when he promised that he wouldn't tell, they said that he could play with them.

Rashnu could not contain his excitement. The boys from the village told him to follow them back over the wall. Rashnu stopped dead still. He said that he never meant that. He said that he meant that he would like to play with them in the palace grounds. It wasn't to be, though. They told him that they only came in here when they were playing dares. They never stopped to play in here. It was too dangerous. They made their way back to the wall, and with a pounding heart, Rashnu followed them. He could barely believe it. In no time at all, he was standing barefoot on the other side of the wall with the boys from the village. They asked him what he wanted to play, but he was too excited to talk properly. He just kind of shrugged his shoulders. The children from the village decided that they would go down to the river to swim. They weren't allowed to go there by themselves because it was dangerous, so they went and asked Abdullah's father. He was the only adult that would ever come with them. He was busy doing some work, but he left straight away and said that he would come with them because swimming in the river sounded much more fun than working. They all went off to the river together and laughed and joked as they went. When they got there, the boys jumped off the rocks and splashed into the water. Abdullah's father jumped in with them and threw them about in the water. Rashnu sat on the rocks and looked at them. His face lit up as he saw the boys being thrown through the air. They all called him to come in but he told them that he didn't know how to swim. They all

found it hard to believe. Everybody

knew how to swim, or at least that's

what they thought. None of the children could have guessed this, but Rashnu had never tried to swim before. This was the first time that he had ever been to the river. They all shouted at him to come in. Rashnu shook his head, but they kept on calling him. In the end, Rashnu thought that if everybody else could do it, then it surely couldn't be that hard. He stood up and stepped back. He took a few short paces forward and jumped far out into the water. He went lower and lower into the water and, when he realised just how deep it was, he began to panic. He splashed out and kicked for all he was worth. When he finally managed to scramble his way up to the surface all of the boys and Abdullah's father clapped their hands. Rashnu was far from pleased with himself though. When he reached the top he realised that his turban had come loose from his head and was lying at

the bottom of the riverbed.

Rashnu began to panic. He

scrambled in a clumsy, splashing kind

of way to the side and shouted for help. He asked the other boys if they could swim down and find his turban for him. He couldn't explain the full story to them, but they were actually looking for one of the most precious jewels in the whole wide world. One by one, they dived down and tried to retrieve it. But one by one their efforts ended in failure. Rashnu began to cry. He couldn't believe how foolish he had been. He had been away from the palace far too long. Soon the servants would miss him and raise the guards. If his father were to find out what he had done, he would raise the whole army to look for him. The thought of his father finding out that he had lost the most precious jewel in the royal household filled him with untold fear. He decided that he had to tell Abdullah's father that the turban was very precious and ask him to try and retrieve it. Abdullah's father smiled at Rashnu and told him not to worry. He put his arm around Rashnu's shoulders and tousled his hair.

With that, he swam down and searched around the riverbed, but he came back up with nothing. Rashnu was distraught. He was beside himself with worry and fear. He told Abdullah's father that he was the prince, but he didn't dare tell him that the most expensive jewel in the world was sewn into his turban. Abdullah's father tried again to retrieve the turban, but it was no use. He couldn't find it. Rashnu begged him to try one more time. He told him it was a special turban and that it was a gift from the King. Abdullah's father said that he would try one more time. He took a deep breath and dived. He swam down to the riverbed once more and felt around for the shiny cloth. The boys waited at the top. He was down there for a long time. The boys wondered how long he could stay down there without breathing. Then he came back up to the surface with a huge thrust. He gasped for air to get some oxygen back into his lungs. Rashnu shouted at him to find out if he had found his turban. Abdullah's father shook his head and had a very serious look on his face.

Then his eyes opened wide as he said, "Look what I've got!" and he held the turban up above his head.

As he passed the turban over to

Rashnu, he couldn't help but notice the

beautiful jewels sewn into it. Rashnu

panicked.

"You can't steal them," he said. "My father will send his finest warriors to hunt you down if you steal them".

All of the children and Abdullah's father fell silent. Abdullah's father pressed the turban into Rashnu's hand.

"I may be a poor working man," he said "but I am not a thief. I have never done anything to you but show you kindness. I am the man that has just saved your precious jewel for you and returned it safely."

Rashnu felt dreadful. "Forgive me, forgive me," he said.

They all walked back to the palace wall. Abdullah's father helped Rashnu back up onto the wall and walked away. Rashnu apologised again, but Abdullah's father just walked away in silence. Abdullah went with him. The boys who stayed behind told Rashnu not to worry. They said that Abdullah's father was nobody for a prince to worry about. Rashnu didn't agree. He said that Abdullah's father was a good man and a good father. He said that he was a good citizen as well and he said that the King would get to know of it.

Rashnu thought long and hard about his adventure. He thought about how brave he had been, he thought about how deceitful he had been, and he thought about how foolish he had been.

Rashnu spent many long hours in

despair. He lay on his bed and sent his servants away. He had always tried to be the kind of son that would make his father proud of him, but his recent actions were disgraceful. He had let his father down badly, but worse than that, he had let himself down. The one thing that troubled him most was the way that he had treated Abdullah's father. He had treated Rashnu with nothing but kindness and, in return, Rashnu had accused him of being a

thief. He reproached himself

tirelessly. He asked himself the same

questions over and over again. How

could he have said such things to a good and honest man? How could he think the worst of someone who had treated him so well? The prince made up his mind. He was going to be braver than he had ever been. He was determined to tell his father, the King, how shamefully he had acted. At their next weekly meeting, Rashnu determined that he would bow down before the King and confess all of the things that he had done.

The hours and days passed slowly as Rashnu waited patiently for his weekly audience with his father. He could think of nothing else. He practised the words that he was going to say over and over again. Each time that he said the words in his mind, they became increasingly difficult to repeat.

Rashnu woke up very early indeed on the day of the meeting. Before he could blink an eye, his mind started to rehearse his confession. Rashnu washed his face and paced up and down the huge high-walled room that was his bedroom. The servants brought him cheese and bread for his breakfast. They served it to him on huge silver plates with freshly cut fruit that decorated the outside of the plates in bright colours. Rashnu thanked them but told them that he could eat nothing today and asked them to take the food away.

The servants were obedient. They bowed their heads and returned the food to the kitchen.

Rashnu continued to pace about his

room. He took deep breaths and said a prayer. He put his hands together and closed his eyes.

"Please help me to be strong and brave and help me to do the right thing."

When the time came for Rashnu to visit his father, Rashnu's senior teachers came to collect him. Rashnu was inspected. His teachers made sure that he was clean and tidy and then they led the way. As they walked towards his father's throne room, Rashnu felt an increasing tension in his stomach. His mouth went dry and the palms of his hands went wet. He had to work hard to control his breathing. It came to his mind that it would be easier to flee back to his room and hide there, but Rashnu was determined to be strong.

When they reached the big double doors that opened into the King's throne room, the most senior of the teachers knocked upon the door and they waited. The wait seemed to last for hours. Eventually, the great doors opened and Rashnu was summoned to advance towards his father.

As Rashnu walked towards his father, his emotions spilled over. Tears came pouring from his eyes and his shoulders shook beyond control. He ran towards his father and fell down at his feet.

"Father, father, please forgive

me," he cried. "I have been so so bad. I have been a bad son and I have let you down."

The King was shocked at what he saw and he beckoned the servants to help Rashnu to his feet. Rashnu fell towards the King and threw his arms around him. He buried his head in his father's chest and sobbed.

"I have done very wrong things," he said. "I have been sneaking onto the roof and looking at the village children as they climbed the trees and I went to see them and I was only going to stay inside but they asked me to go with them and I told them I was a servant boy and we went to the river and I lost my turban and Abdullah's father found it for me and I said such dreadful, dreadful, things to him, father and I'm so ashamed and I'll never be able to ask him to forgive me and I'm so sorry, father, and I'll never do anything wrong again and I promise to be better in the future and I'll never do anything ·bad again. I promise."

The King and the teachers and the servants were shocked. Nobody, it seemed, knew what to say and everybody looked at each other.

The King didn't quite know what to do with the young boy whose tears were soaking his fine royal clothes. He gently patted him on the shoulders and on his arms.

Rashnu said, "Oh, thank you, father, thank you," and he reached up and kissed his father on the cheek.

The King smiled. He touched his cheek as though he expected the kiss to come away on his fingers.

The servants and the teachers seemed to let out a sigh as though they had been forced to hold their breath, whilst the unbelievable scene unfolded before them.

When the drama of the moment

subsided, Rashnu explained everything to his father. The King was very surprised at what he heard but he was not angry. He was rather proud of his son. He said that it was he who should be saying sorry to the young prince.

"This is my fault," the King said. "I should never have kept you hidden away inside the palace walls. It's not fair for a young boy to grow up without other children to play with. No. This is clearly a fault of my own making. I was far too concerned with preparing you for the future and not nearly concerned enough about the present. "From now on," the King said, "things will be different. You will be able to play with other children. This is good. You should learn about people. One day you will be the ruler of a great land and it is right that you should know the people of your land. Your sorrow does you credit. You were not caught but you confessed. You make me proud".

In the course of the next day, Rashnu was summoned back to his father's throne room. This was a very rare occurrence indeed and Rashnu was delighted to be seeing his father again so soon.

When Rashnu arrived at his father's throne room, his eyes lit up at the sight that met them. Standing by the side of his father was Abdullah. He was smiling a huge broad smile and

Abdullah's father stood there too. He was smiling every bit as broadly as his son.

Rashnu could hardly believe it. He walked towards his father and bowed down before him and then he walked towards Abdullah's father and knelt down before him.

"I am pleased to see you again. I did a bad thing by telling you things that were not true. When I accused you of stealing the royal jewels I was

very wrong indeed. You had only ever

shown me such kindness and I am very

sorry for my actions. Please forgive me."

Abdullah's father smiled more warmly than ever and told the young prince to be upstanding. "Anybody can say things in haste that they later regret," he said, "especially when they have just lost the most precious jewel in the world."

Everybody, including the King, laughed, and Rashnu felt a wave of happiness sweep over him. He had never seen the King laugh before and he liked it.

The King spoke again. "Abdullah's father has kindly agreed to come and work for us," he said. "You will travel around this land and meet people. Other children. Good people, like Abdullah's father here, and you will be safe. You will be guided by an honest man and you will have good friends. I know this because Abdullah's father here will be your guide."

The King sat back on his throne and clasped his hands together. Rashnu threw his arms around Abdullah and then threw his arms around Abdullah's father. Then Rashnu became so overjoyed, he rushed to his father and threw his arms around him too. The King was surprised by his son's actions, he was not used to receiving affection, but he didn't mind...

In fact, he liked it.

Also by the same author...

Harriet
the
Horrible

E.R.Reilly

Harriet is a lovely little girl- that is until she
gets upset. Then she dreams up wonderfully
wicked plans to get her own back...Watch out!
That's when nice little Harriet becomes
... Harriet the Horrible!

Harriet the Horrible in Best Friends

E.R.Reilly

Harriet and Salty have always got up to lots of mischief but now they are joined by a new girl in school.
Colleen is Harriet's new best friend and toether they have a very special mission in life...

One boy,
One dream,
One club...

E.R.Reilly

This is the story of one boy's dream to be a professional footballer. It is a roller-coaster ride of a book that reaches out to everybody who has ever had a dream.

Contact us to order any of these titles.

SANTIAGO PRESS
PO BOX 8808
BIRMINGHAM
B30 2LR

santiago@reilly19.freeserve.co.uk